To the awesome Michael Levine, my good friend and talented
music producer, and his groovy family, Bonnie, Eden, and Emet. —E.L.

To Amy Krouse Rosenthal, with love and appreciation. —T.L.

Text copyright © 2016 by Eric Litwin
Illustrations copyright © 2016 by Tom Lichtenheld

Printed in Malaysia 108 • First edition, September 2016
The text type is set in Clarendon.
Book design by Tom Lichtenheld and Patti Ann Harris

Groovy Joe
Ice Cream & Dinosaurs

by Eric Litwin

Illustrated by
Tom Lichtenheld

ORCHARD BOOKS • NEW YORK
An Imprint of Scholastic Inc.

Groovy Joe saw something yummy.

Groovy Joe started
rubbing his tummy.

Groovy Joe was living the dream.

He had a spoon
and a tub of
ice cream.

And he started
to sing...

Love
my doggy
ice cream!

A *LITTLE* dinosaur
stomped into the room.

He glared at the ice cream and took out a…

Spoon!

He put on a bib!
He pulled up a chair!

What did Joe say?

"It's awesome to share!"

And everyone sang...

Love my doggy ice cream!

Love my doggy ice cream!

OH NO.!!

A *BIG* dinosaur
burst into the room.

He glared at the ice cream
and took out a...

Spoon!

He put on a bib!
He pulled up a chair!

What did Joe say?

"It's awesome to share!"

And everyone sang...

dinosaur spit

A **HUGE** dinosaur
smashed into the room.

She glared at the ice cream
and took out a...

Spoon!

She put on a bib!

She pulled up a chair!

What did
Joe say?

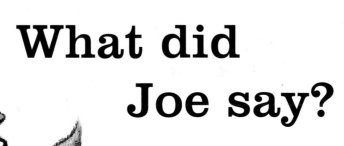

"It's awesome to share!"

And everyone sang...

The tub was empty.
The ice cream
was through.

So the dinosaurs glared
at you-know-who.

What can Joe do?

He turned over the tub and made it a drum.

Groovy Joe beat out a **rum-tum-a-tum-tum.**

The dinosaurs laughed.

They rose from their chairs.

They started to dance.

"It's awesome to share!"

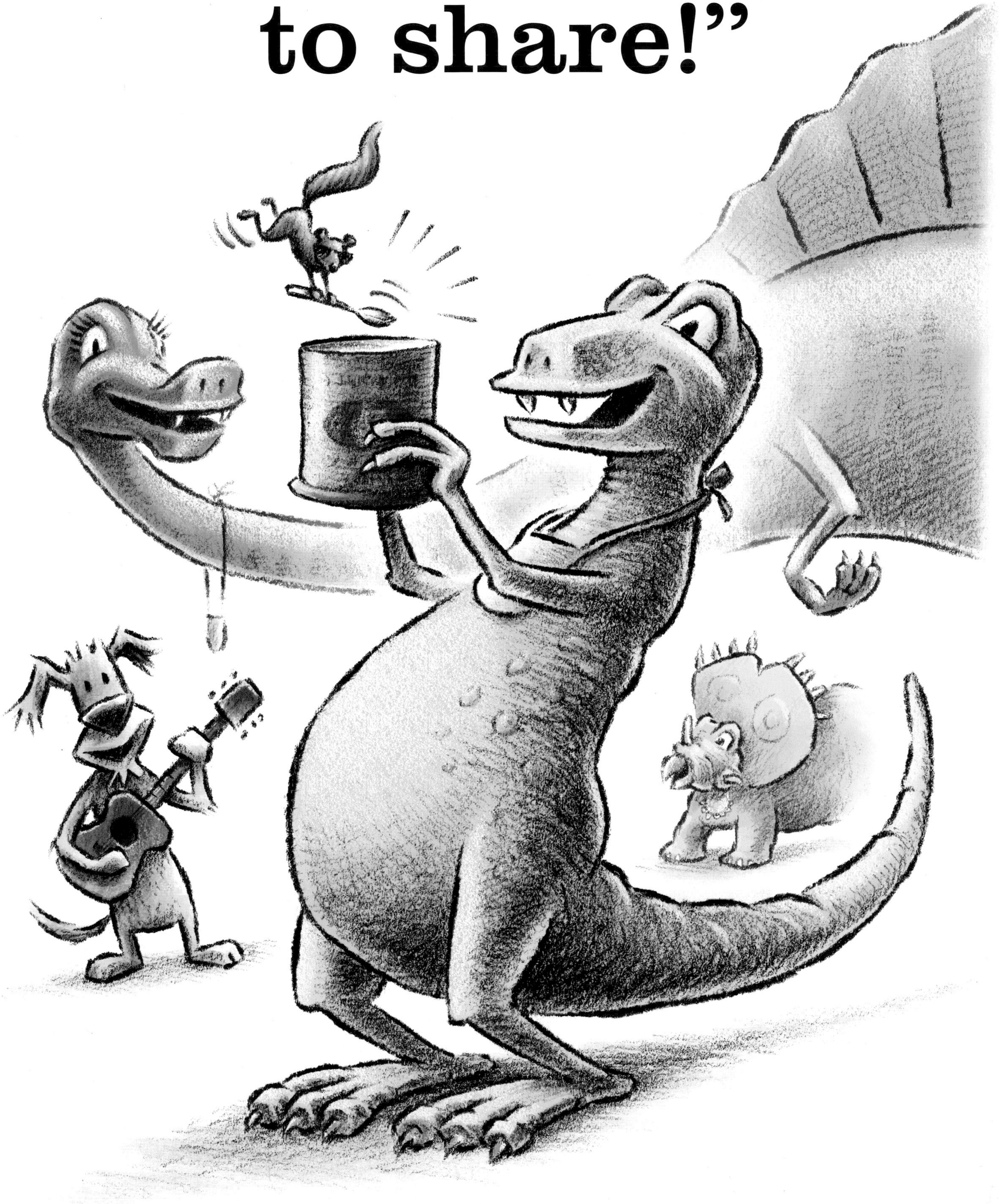

The Groovy Dance
by Eric Litwin

Go here, go there
here, there, here, there
Go here, go there
here, there, here, there
Get Groovy, uh-huh
Get Groovy, uh-huh
Get Groovy, uh-huh
Call it out! Get Groovy!
Go hi, go low
hi, low, hi, low
Go hi, go low
hi, low, hi, low
Get Groovy, uh-huh
Get Groovy, uh-huh
Get Groovy, uh-huh
Call it out! Get Groovy!
Jump in, jump out
in, out, in, out
Jump in, jump out
in, out, in, out
Get Groovy, uh-huh
Get Groovy, uh-huh
Get Groovy, uh-huh
Call it out! Get Groovy!